Sherlock Holmes

and

The Missing Helmets

Teresa Wimmer

Paperback ISBN 978-1-78092-743-5
ePub ISBN 978-1-78092-744-2
PDF ISBN 978-1-78092-745-9

Published in the UK by MX Publishing
335 Princess Park Manor, Royal Drive,
London, N11 3GX
www.mxpublishing.co.uk

Cover design by www.staunch.com

A special thank you to my best friend Anna and my former English teacher Mr. B.

Prologue

My friend Sherlock Holmes was a strange man. I often saw him get strange looks for what he did and said. But none of that had ever mattered to him. In his world, there was only his work. He loved his work so much that he wouldn't have survived without it. Sherlock Holmes, the consulting detective, wasn't searching for crime. No, the crimes went searching for him.

Unfortunately it had taken me too long to realize this truth. We had been flatmates for about a year. Only one year, you'd think, but it had been the most exciting year of my life. Even though I would often have welcomed some peace and quiet, I was glad for the cases I had solved with Sherlock. He was just the sort of man I had needed as a friend and it seemed to me that he needed me, too. I couldn't always comprehend why, but I was certain he did need my help and was happy to have me by his side.

One day in February of 2012 I was quite fed up with all the running, Sherlock's moods and the constant fear of being killed by some dangerous criminal. I thought I was ready to take a holiday, but I hadn't been counting on Sherlock's magnetic attraction towards crimes.

Chapter One: The Skiing Trip

I entered the flat of 221B Baker Street, which was Sherlock's and my home, with my girlfriend Lisa. I was glad to have escaped the rainy streets of London. It was late-afternoon and the air outside was cool.

Lisa and I went into the living-room after I had hung up our coats. This space was more than just the heart of our flat; it was an office where Sherlock and I welcomed our clients, a laboratory and a comfortable place to find some rest all at once. Scattered throughout the room were parts of Sherlock's experiments and some newspaper clippings. Sherlock, with his black hair and his pale face, had rolled himself up into a ball in his favourite armchair and was staring angrily at the screen of his laptop. His eyes were narrow and his mouth was a thin line. Rage had welled up inside him, ready to burst outwards any second. I acted as if I were oblivious to this.

"Hey Sherlock!" I called. No reaction.

"Sherlock" I tried again.

"Shut up, John!" Sherlock hissed.

He was angry and moody just as I had guessed, but what was worse, he had been unfriendly like that for days!

"Oh, is he working on a case?" whispered Lisa.

Oh no! This was the wrong question, and it brought Sherlock's temper to the breaking point.

"NO!" shouted Sherlock, "NO, NO, NO. I have no case. I have nothing to do. I'm bored." Yes, he was bored and I knew this bored mood of his quite well.

A normal person would have welcomed periods of peace, without work and without the daily rush, but not Sherlock Holmes. These times without work were like poison is his veins.

"It's alright, Sherlock, calm down. You've just solved a case. You've just been working too much in the last weeks." I said.

"No. It's not enough." Sherlock disagreed "No one is contacting me. Come on. Something has to happen...something bad and mysterious would be nice..." Suddenly he snapped the laptop shut, stood up and started pacing around. He put his long fingers together and examined Lisa and me closely.

"John, you came here with her for a special reason. You look happy, you were holding her hand when you entered, but she isn't wearing a new ring...You've just decided to do something, you want to take a trip. Where to? It's winter, you will need to pack a lot of warm clothes, it's going to be expensive..." he said in his usual, fast deducing speed "Ha! You are going to take a skiing trip with Lisa. How nice, John."

I didn't even want to ask how Sherlock knew this. He would only make a show out of it again.

"Of course you are right," *as always*, I added in my mind, "we are taking a couple's holiday in the German Alps. We'll stay in the beautiful town of Lenggries."

"Have a good time," said Sherlock and turned away.

"Thanks, and just so you know, you'll have to look after yourself for a week. Do you think you can manage that?"

"Sure, John" he said crisply and sat down again, this time grabbing his violin to play a little tune. It wasn't a pleasant tune. It was uncomfortably high-pitched and lacking in structure. I wasn't so sure Sherlock would cope without me.

"So since this is all clear, can we have dinner now?" asked Lisa. I thanked Lisa silently for that change of topic. We both went into the kitchen and prepared the meal.

Dinner was a quiet affair. Sherlock was in a bad mood and not for any small talk. Lisa and I chatted a little about our trip. Lisa was very delighted for the trip to Germany, where she had never been before, and I was glad to see her so happy. The entire time, her happiness reminded me of Sherlock's foul mood, and so I contemplated an opportunity for making

Sherlock feel better. He would definitely need a case while he was alone, but he was so quick in solving them that he might even need a great many cases to stay stable for an entire week. Or else he would find something else to do...

Suddenly I had an idea. This would, of course, reduce Lisa's happiness, but Sherlock was in worse condition than she was and I couldn't just leave him alone during times like these and so I said:

"Sherlock, would you perhaps like to come with us? That way you would have something to do and you wouldn't be alone."

Lisa made a face at this, just as I had guessed.

Sherlock's answer was nonetheless: "Me, skiing? Definitely not."

"Why not? It would do you some good to get away from London for a few days. Catch yourself some fresh air; you are always stuck to the city."

"I do not ski. That's why not."

"And why won't you *try* skiing? Skiing is a lot of fun."

"Skiing is boring and normal."

"Have you ever even been skiing?"

"No, I don't need to." That was just so typical for him.

"Oh, come on Sherlock, you don't know that that's true. Why

not just give it a try?"

"What should Sherlock try?" asked Mrs Hudson as she entered the kitchen. Mrs Hudson was a lovely elderly woman who always sort of made you feel as though you were her child.

I looked up and answered: "He should come on a skiing trip with Lisa and me. I think the fresh air and the sport would do him a great deal of good"

Mrs Hudson scrutinized Sherlock critically and said: "John's right. You really need to get out of here, dear. Look at yourself! How pale you are!"

I was very grateful for Mrs Hudson's support in this matter and smiled: "See? Just come with us. I promise it won't be boring."

"No, I won't come. I'll just annoy you and Lisa."

I had to laugh to myself. "Hey! Sherlock, you have never been that considerate. Don't start now."

"No, I don't want to leave Baker Street. Perhaps there will be a case soon." He'd come up with better excuses before.

"Sherlock, you are so stubborn. You need to do something for your health. Get out of here, or I'll throw you out. You can't just sit around and do nothing but wait for a case." said Mrs Hudson angrily and I was certain she meant every single word.

She and I continued talking to him until he got so annoyed that he agreed to come.

"This will be fun," I said.

Mrs Hudson added: "I expect you to take some photos as proof that you really went skiing!" Sherlock managed to smile just then and I knew he was alright. But on the other hand, Lisa had been quiet the entire time. She didn't like the idea of Sherlock coming with us, but was polite enough to not admit this in front of him. I knew that we would fight over it later. I truly loved her and wanted our relationship to work. But at this particular moment, Sherlock was more important and I was sure this trip would be pleasant and would hopefully pass *without* much action.

Chapter Two: The Instructor

The following morning was full of chaos. Once everything had been packed; Sherlock and I grabbed ourselves a cab and drove off to Lisa's flat. Sherlock stayed in the car while I went up to fetch her. I greeted Lisa with a kiss as usual. We had had an argument over Sherlock coming with us, but in the end she agreed that we could still enjoy our couple's holiday even if Sherlock was in Lenggries, too. He would stay out of our way most of the time and so, in the end, Lisa was content with our trip after all.

The weather in London was cold and cloudy, but luckily there was neither rain nor storm. Heathrow was crawling with people. Some were happily off on holiday, while others were hurriedly rushing to business meetings. I relaxed a little once we had reached our seats and the plane had taken off.

Five hours later we arrived at our hotel in Lenggries. Lenggries was a beautiful little Bavarian town with a skiing area close by. It was about an hour's drive south from Munich. The town was full of tourists and skiing businesses. The houses looked as though they had come from another time. They had inclined roofs, wooden balconies and some even had beautiful pictures of majestic stags or saints who were supposed to protect the people living inside, painted on the walls. Our hotel was very lovely. It seemed like an oversized Bavarian hut with snow hanging from the rooftop, which made the building look very romantic. The rooms themselves were very comfortable and the walls were adorned with pictures of the mountains.

After a short tour through the hotel, Sherlock, Lisa and I decided to have dinner. This was my second time in Germany. My parents, my brother, and I had spent a few days in Berlin when I was ten, but Bavaria was completely different. Especially the food. We had bread dumplings and roast pork for dinner and it was delicious. Of course we also drank the famous Bavarian beer. It tasted better than some British sorts of beer, but not all of them. It just tasted much more of herbs and such. But I really wasn't an expert where beer was concerned anyway.

The conversation over dinner was mostly small-talk about our surroundings.

"I've never seen such huge mountains before", said Lisa.

Sherlock replied: "And it really is kind of impressive to be surrounded by so much snow. I really would like to know how one survives an avalanche."

I shook my head at that comment and said: "This is an experiment you'd better not try."

Later Lisa and I visited a bar without Sherlock, who had gone on to inspect the streets around our hotel. He knows every single street in London, but now he was in an area he'd never been in before. Of course he would make a street map in his master mind.

The next day after breakfast, Lisa and I appeared in the sitting room with ski suits and couldn't believe our eyes. "Sherlock, you can't seriously want to ski like that?!" I exclaimed. Sherlock was wearing his usual long coat, thin gloves, and a scarf, but no helmet or waterproof trousers. This outfit would have been proper for a walk, but not for skiing.

"Why not? I'm wearing ski boots and that's all I need," answered Sherlock calmly. "Sherlock! There's snow outside and snow is wet and you'll catch a cold soon if you don't wear something that's waterproof and warm." I was really distressed on behalf of Sherlock's stupidity. For being such a clever guy, he certainly behaved irresponsibly sometimes.

"Why do you always talk to him as if he were a small child?" asked Lisa amused. She choked down a little laughter, but I didn't think it was funny at all.

"Because he *is* a small child in so many ways!" I shouted. Lisa made an offended face because she didn't like being shouted at and I quickly apologised to her. Sherlock remained calm. "I will ski without this clown costume or I will go straight back home." What a threat!

I knew it was no good arguing with him, so we took the bus to the cable car. I had been on a few skiing trips before, but Lisa and Sherlock had no experience in skiing, and so I had organised a personal instructor for them.

After a short walk, we entered the skiing school. It was a huge building set next to the ski lifts with a sign that read "Skischule Lengriess".

"Err, Sherlock, you can speak German, can't you?" I asked and looked at Sherlock.

"Yes, I can. Don't they speak English?"

"Not everybody speaks English here, I guess. So please go on, and ask for Mr Gerg. He's our instructor."

Sherlock stepped up to the information desk and said in German: "Guten Tag, mein Freund John Watson hat um einen Lehrer gebeten. Er heißt Herr Gerg."[1]

„Einen Moment bitte,"[2] the woman at the counter said. She called something out in German into the room behind her and soon a man came in. He was wearing a yellow ski suit, boots and a helmet. I couldn't make out all of his face because of the helmet, but he appeared to be very young, maybe about twenty-five. He seemed very athletic, judging from the way he stood. But otherwise, there was very little for me to observe. Sherlock, on the other hand, looked at him very closely. He absorbed all the details of the instructor in his usual way. I knew his deduction would soon follow, so I gave the instructor my hand immediately and said: "Hello, I'm Doctor John Watson. This is my girlfriend Lisa Clark and my friend Sherlock Holmes."

"Nice to meet you. I'm Gerd Gerg. I hope you excuse that my English isn't so good." He said in a very strong accent. Just like every German, he pronounced the English words quite harshly.

"Of course that's fine," I said and Lisa nodded in a friendly manner. Sherlock, on the other hand, showed no reaction at all. Perhaps Germans were more difficult to deduce.

"So, then. Let's start," said Mr Gerg enthusiastically and we went outside with our skis over our shoulders.

"This is the easiest slope here." He explained, pointing to the slope ahead of us. "We'll start with putting on the skis. It isn't actually as easy as it may appear", he went on and showed us how to put the shoes into the bindings. Lisa had some difficulties and I helped her, but Sherlock was very quick to stand straight up on his skis. "Very good, Mr Holmes," said Mr Gerg.

Sherlock smiled and replied: "Thank you, but it's really very easy. I've watched very closely while others have done it. I know you want to make everything as good as possible because this is your first year as a graduated instructor. You need this job because you have been fired as a personal fitness trainer. You probably lost it because you were having an affair with one of your clients and you recently got beaten up by her husband. You do like skiing, but you don't like ski suits. You're uncomfortable in them. Most likely you live close by and began to ski at a very early age. You still live with your mother because she says she needs you. But you want to move out, so you need all the money you can get. So you take on the foreign students because they pay you more. Because of this, you have to be extremely nice to us so that we will give greater tips. Am I wrong?"

Of course I had been wrong about Germans being more difficult to deduce. Sherlock had made his deduction of the young instructor just as I had feared. In spite of my annoyance, I never got used to the brilliance of Sherlock's deductions. Every time I asked myself why I hadn't seen all of these facts the first time I looked at someone.

Nonetheless, I hoped the German hadn't understood everything. Sherlock had been speaking very rapidly again. But Mr Gerg had clearly understood the main content, because he was staring just as stupidly as everyone else who met Sherlock for the first time.

"How can you know all this?" He asked. Sherlock was about to start explaining when I quickly interrupted: "No. Please just ignore this. This is just a game of his."

But Sherlock was unstoppable: "In the skiing school there was just one folder with your name on it and the year 2012. The other instructors have one folder for each year. So freshly graduated. You need money because you have an iPhone 4, but the new iPhone 4S is already on the market and someone like you always needs the latest versions of everything."

Sherlock took a short break and the young Gerg asked: "What about my job as a fitness coach?"

"Ah, well, it's so easy. Even under your thick jacket, I can see you've got really pronounced muscles. So maybe you go to the fitness centre regularly, or you work at a fitness centre. But you don't have much money, so why would you waste it in a fitness studio? Therefore you work there. You look, well, women may call it attractive," Sherlock smirked. "So you would probably work mostly with women. But why did you lose your job? You must have been fired. You earned good wages - otherwise you wouldn't even have an iPhone 4- and wouldn't have gone voluntarily. You've got a green mark on your cheekbone, so you must have been beaten very hard. The connection is clear, isn't it? Working with women, fired and beaten? You had an affair with bad consequences."

"And what about Mami?"

"Mami? I'm correct there too, am I not? Well, the pocket of your jacket is open, so I can see you've got a homemade sandwich with cucumbers and mustard. You don't make such sandwiches by yourself and you don't have a girlfriend. Bingo, your mother made the sandwiches. They aren't in good condition because you stuffed them harshly into your pocket, therefore you want to get away from her. You want to get away from her because living with your mother really isn't cool and your mother fusses too much about you. And by the way it's common knowledge that tourists pay more money than locals. Everything clear?"

Mr Gerg was in deep shock after this speech. "What are you?" he asked.

I felt bad for him. It wasn't a nice feeling to learn that some guy you had never met before knew everything about you, but it was still kind of rude to ask what Sherlock was.

"'What'? That is none of your business, but let's just say I have a highly-efficient brain," Sherlock explained, and then the deduction was mercifully over.

Sherlock remained normal for the rest of the day. He was really quick at learning to ski and soon left Lisa and I to ski alone for a while. Lisa wasn't making such good progress, so we stayed at the easiest slope all day. I was secretly happy to spend some time away from Sherlock because he was really getting on my nerves and I suppose he was getting on Lisa's as well. Mr Gerg was still very friendly, but he seemed to be glad for Sherlock's absence, too.

Chapter Three: Many Accidents

After we had finished skiing, Lisa and I went to an après ski party because we had heard that these parties were very popular in skiing regions. We had asked Sherlock to come with us, but he didn't want to. He went to play the violin in his hotel room instead.

The après ski party was in a huge tent only a few minutes away from the skiing school. Loud music was coming out of it. Inside it was very cosy. There was a crowded dance floor and a bar offering all sorts of drinks, some drinks I had never heard of.

"Oh John, it's good to do something without Sherlock! You know, now it's just the two of us…" said Lisa happily and kissed me. "Yeah," I answered and smiled at her before going to buy us some drinks. We were drinking Bavarian beer and listening to "Ski fahren" by Wolfgang Ambros. "They have really good music here, but it's a pity that I can't understand the lyrics. This song is about skiing I suppose," said Lisa and moved to the music. A little while later both Lisa and I were dancing with many other people in the dim light. But I wasn't a very good dancer so I soon gave up and went to the bar to drink some coke. I was ordering in English when a barkeeper said to me: "He, du Ami. Mia san hier in Bayern und i versteh dei G'schwafel net."[3]

Luckily another man stepped in to help me and said: "Sorry, mister. My dad can't speak English. May I help you?"

"Yes, please. I wanted to order a coke."

"Eine Cola bitte für den Herrn hier."

"Aha, das wollte der also sagen. Diese Amis sind schon komisch. Hier ist seine Cola. Sag ihm, dass sie 2,80 kostet und ich will Euros, keine Dollars," replied the bar-keeper.

I understood nothing of their conversation which was good for me, I suppose. But of course I had made out that the bar-keeper wasn't being nice. The friendly man translated: "Here is your coke. It costs 2.80 Euros. Do you have Euros, mister? My dad doesn't take dollars." I had to laugh at this. "Yeah, sure. Here they are. I'm from England by the way and not from the USA. We've got Pounds."

"Sorry, mister. I hope I haven't offended you.", said the young man wistfully, his English was much better than that of Mr Gerg.

"No, no, it's all right. It must be difficult for foreigners to hear the difference between British English and American English." I responded and smiled.

"Yes, you are right."

The two of us talked for a while about languages, countries and skiing.

Suddenly the word "accidents" dropped into the conversation. "Err, sorry what did you just say about accidents?" I asked.

"Oh, yes. The accidents… There have been five accidents in the last five days. One accident each day. Skiing accidents, you know. Very bad ones. Two people are still in critical condition," the man explained.

"And this is unusual? I mean there aren't always so many accidents, are there? I have heard that skiing can be very dangerous if you're not careful enough. Especially since so many people are out on the slopes."

"Well, sure it's dangerous, but not that much. Usually there's just one bad accident a week, not five!"

"Is there a specific place where these accidents have occurred?"

"Not really. But it's always here around Lenggries, and all the accidents happened near trees. But that's understandable, because many accidents are caused by collisions."

"Has anyone been investigating how these accidents happened?" I asked. I was starting to get really interested. Maybe this was a case for Sherlock!

"Well, no. I mean there are no police involved, but there's a reason why these accidents ended so badly. None of the victims were wearing a helmet." We both fell into silence, contemplating what had just been said.

At this moment Lisa appeared at my side. "Hey, John! What's going on? I want to go back to the hotel," she said.

"Oh, I just had a nice chat with… sorry?" I replied and then looked questioningly at my conversation partner. "I'm Sepp. Hello." The son of the barkeeper introduced himself for the first time.

"Hi, nice to meet you. I'm Lisa and this is John," Lisa said to Sepp before turning to me again. "What about going back to the hotel? I'm tired." I could see that she was suppressing a yawn.

"Okay, let's go. Bye, Sepp. Thanks for your help earlier and for the chat."

"Bye. It was nice to talk to you, too."

Lisa and I returned to the hotel and we soon were asleep in our bed. On our way in, we found out that Sherlock had gotten into an argument with his neighbour over him playing the violin. Apparently this neighbour wasn't as accustomed to Sherlock's habits as I was. Playing the violin at three o'clock in the morning was common business in 221b Baker Street. Sherlock had gone to sleep soon after the row, which had at least kept him quiet.

Chapter Four: The New Accident

The next morning I woke up early and went quietly out of the room. I met up with Sherlock in the lounge.

"Morning, Sherlock!"

"Good morning, John," murmured Sherlock. He was sitting in front of his laptop checking to see if he had received any emails.

I ordered some tea and sat down next to him saying, " You don't have to look for a case. I think I have something inter esting for you."

"Hm", was Sherlock's only reaction.

"Won't you listen to me? " I asked desperately.

"Okay, John. Tell me your story." Sherlock seemed annoyed. He liked having me participate in his plans and I knew he thought highly of me, but he still always acted superior, as though my stories could never be as good as his. Most of the time he was right. My life without Sherlock was simple and …dull. I smiled to myself because I knew Sherlock would really be glad for this accident-story: "Well, I met this guy at the party yesterday. He told me about five accidents in this area…" I continued and told everything I knew.

While he was listening, Sherlock's mood changed. He grew very interested.

"And he told me that none of the victims had worn a helmet. You see Sherlock... you really should wear a helmet. Skiing is too dangerous without one."

"Sure, sure, I'll go to the shop right now. Meet you later at the skiing school." Sherlock stood up and walked away. I sighed, relieved. Firstly, I was sure Sherlock had now been set into action again and out of his hole of depression and secondly, I thought Sherlock had, for once listened to me and was now on his way to buy a skiing helmet.

Lisa and I arrived at the skiing school at nine o'clock. Sherlock was already there, ready to go. Just like the day before, he was wearing his coat, gloves and ski boots, but he had... "No helmet, Sherlock?!" I tried to stay calm.

Sherlock smiled and said "Why should I have a helmet, John?"

"What... because you said that you would go to the shop. You didn't buy a helmet?" I sighed.

"No, John. I bought a newspaper and gathered more information about these accidents. What's the problem?"

"I thought that you had listened to me and that you would do what I told you! But as always, you just don't care! Sherlock, skiing without a helmet is deadly dangerous!" I shouted. So much for staying calm.

Sherlock laughed "Oh, John. Life is always deadly dangerous for me." With these words, the argument ended.

We all mastered the easiest slope this day and Mr Gerg introduced us to some slopes higher up the mountain. Skiing there was really a challenge, but we all did well and I really began to enjoy the speed of going down hill. The wind rushed past my ears and the landscape flashed by. There were lots of people on the slopes and you really needed to be careful not to crash into someone or something. I admired little children at the age of about five years skiing as if they had been born to stand on skis. Mr Gerg seemed to be such a natural talent, but maybe it was just an advantage of growing up near the Alps. I simply tried to follow his example as well as I could, always keeping a worrying eye on Lisa, who seemed to be having some trouble.

Suddenly, a crowd of people materialized in the middle of the slope. About a hundred people had gathered and were watching something happening in front of them. We slowly drew nearer to the scene.

Sherlock arrived first and immediately began to study everything around him. Then Mr Gerg came. He took off his skis and attempted to call for order. Lisa and I arrived last. I managed to catch a glimpse of a man lying in the snow, blood pouring from his head. Paramedics in skiing gear came running and the man was concealed from our view.

It soon became clear that a new accident had occurred.

The people were all shouting at the same time and no one was listening to Mr Gerg, the other skiing instructors and paramedics telling them to remain calm.

But one woman was shouting louder than everyone else. She screamed so loud it was hurting my ears. She screamed as if she were in deep pain and to my astonishment, she was doing this in English.

The paramedics had moved to the side a bit and we were once again able to see the injured man. He looked very pale. There was little contrast between the white of the snow and his face. As he lay there, wrapped up in a golden emergency blanket to keep him warm, I could see his skis standing beside him but there was no … helmet.

Within minutes a helicopter had landed and more doctors were rushing to the scene of the accident. They placed the injured man on a stretcher and carried him away. The woman went with them, shouting and crying all at once until she, the injured man and the helicopter had left.

Slowly people began to move on. They started skiing again and soon there was no one left at the scene of the accident. No one but Sherlock, of course.

Sherlock had stayed where he had been and got off his skis. I watched him, then left my skis behind too and went after him.

Now he had run straight into a crime scene. Oh, he liked that! Sherlock had gone to the place were the man had lain just minutes ago. The doctors had attempted to cover the blood, but we could still see a few red stains in the white snow. It looked scary.

There was a tree beside the blood which bore no signs of a crash, but had surely been the reason for the accident. Once again I thought about how strange life sometimes was. The tree was so strong that it would kill anyone who crashed into it with enough force, but the tree itself remained unharmed.

"So what do you think Sherlock? It's strange that there have been so many accidents within just one week, isn't it?" I asked.

"Yes, this is getting better and better. A serial accident provocateur! Perhaps these are as good as serial killers. We'll see. Let's go to the hospital." Sherlock said.

Chapter Five: Mr Smith's Death

"Why should we go to the hospital?" asked Lisa.

"We have to check on the injured man. He's a compatriot of ours. He's English," answered Sherlock as he strapped on his skis before heading down the slope. I followed his lead, because I was really getting curious now. Lisa seemed to be undecided for a moment, but then came after us. A few metres short of the valley I heard Lisa shout behind me: "John, stop!"

I immediately came to a halt and looked back. She stopped near me.

"John, what's this all about? Are you and Sherlock playing detective again?" Lisa asked angrily. Of course, she was absolutely right. Sherlock had been on the case since that morning and it had been growing more and more interesting. I really didn't know what to say to Lisa just then.

Well, I had promised her Sherlock wouldn't annoy us and that we would have a nice couple's holiday, but … these accidents had changed everything.

"Yeah, well, you know this latest victim is English…as Sherlock said, and we're responsible for figuring out how this all happened."

"Oh, John. You don't *have* to do anything. You're here on holiday! With me!"

"Sorry, Lisa" I tried to sound like I really meant it, but the truth was that I was not sorry for wanting to solve this crime, but I knew I would be sorry if I didn't go with Sherlock immediately.

So, putting forth a great effort to sound convincing, I said: "Really, I am sorry. But I think I have to go with Sherlock and help him. I'll go to the hospital, but you can have your holiday and go shopping."

"Right! I'll have my holiday right now. And I will have a lot of fun without you! Good bye, and have fun with Sherlock!"

She turned around and skied down the rest of the slope faster than she had ever skied before. Once she had reached the bottom, she unclipped her skis and literally ran away.

I was feeling really depressed and hoped she would talk to me again later. But then I saw Sherlock standing there waiting for me and I quickly caught up with him. We both took our skis back to the hotel and got a cab to the hospital. Luckily, there was just one hospital in this town where victims of skiing accidents where brought, which was about half an hour away. During the ride Sherlock was lost in deep thought and I knew I should not disturb him, so I just sat quietly beside him and gathered my own thoughts.

The hospital was huge and seemed to be very modern, with a reflecting façade made of glass. The familiar smell of disinfectants greeted us as we entered. This smell, clean and uncomfortable, has always reminded me of my days as an army doctor. But I had treated most of the injuries of my comrades in much worse places than this fancy hospital.

Sherlock was headed on his way straight down the hall when a secretary called: "Kann ich Ihnen helfen?"[4] Sherlock muttered something in English. The secretary seemed not to understand him, but let us go anyway. I followed Sherlock in silence, but I was really curious as to how he would get permission to see the injured man. I was certain that he was in intensive care and only family members were allowed to go in there. Formalities such as these were the same in every country.

But he was, after all, Sherlock. He always knew how to tell a good lie.

Soon we arrived in intensive care. Nurses and doctors were running around. Someone shouted an order. Everyone seemed to be in a big hurry. But not chaotically. They all seemed to follow some sort of pattern. I knew from my days as a doctor myself just how tense the nerves are in such emergencies and I silently begged that the injured man would survive.

Sherlock paid no mind to the chaos around him and simply went on. I followed him, of course, but with all the people running around it got pretty difficult to keep up. Suddenly I couldn't see Sherlock ahead of me anymore. I stopped and turned around. He had gone through a door into some sitting room, where there was just one woman seated.

It was the woman who had been screaming at the scene of the accident. She was sobbing terribly and babbling into her handkerchief: "No, no, this is just some bad dream. Oh, George...please."

Sherlock sat down beside her and said: "Sorry, ma'am. Why are you so sad? Can I help you?"

His voice sounded unnaturally friendly to me.

"Oh, thank you. You speak English?"

"Er, yes. I'm from London."

"London? I'm from London, too. It would have been better if we would have stayed in London..." She cried out loudly.

"We? Who do you mean?"

"George", she replied through her tears.

"What's wrong with George?"

"Oh, George...He's... he's dead. He's ...was my husband. He died just an hour ago. Just hours ago he was skiing cheerfully and now..."

"What happened?"

"Well, he had a skiing accident. A helicopter came and brought him to this hospital. I couldn't understand what the doctors in the helicopter were saying and no one had the time or the skills to explain to me in English what was going on. But George looked really bad. And when we arrived here it was already too late. His brain didn't work anymore." She blew her nose in her handkerchief.

"Oh, I'm so very sorry," said Sherlock sincerely, "my condolences."

He let the woman cry a bit more and then asked: "Was George a good skier?"

"Yes, he has...had been skiing since he was a little boy. He is...I mean, he was very good. He never ever had any accidents. But today- I don't know why it happened. First his helmet was stolen, and then this accident..."

"What? His helmet had been stolen? Really?" exclaimed Sherlock, acting as though he were surprised.

"Yes, we had lunch at a restaurant and when we got up to leave his helmet was gone. And I'm absolutely sure it was stolen and not just taken by accident because his name was written on the helmet in golden letters: George Smith. I can't find any sense in stealing a ski helmet. But it really did happen and exactly the same day, this terrible accident happened, too."

Mrs Smith - I had worked out her name during the conversation - was completely at wit's end. She cried and cried. Suddenly, Sherlock stood up and said to me: "Take care of her for a while, I have to find something out."

In the next moment he was gone. I didn't know what to do with Mrs Smith so I sat down in Sherlock's former place and put an arm around her and offered some words to help her calm down a bit. Suddenly, she turned to hug me and began to cry even harder. Her tears soaked my shirt. I held her as best I could and hoped she would let go of me soon. I felt very uncomfortable, but what else was I to do?

I was very glad when Sherlock finally returned half an hour later. We said goodbye to Mrs Smith, who thanked us very warmly for our comfort. She promised us that she would get in touch with her daughter soon. The daughter would take her home to London, and maybe help her mother to cope with Mr Smith's death.

Six: The Help

"Sherlock, tell me, what are you thinking?" I said on our way back to the hotel and an angry Lisa. How would I explain all of this to her?

"John, I don't like to talk about my theories if they are uncertain. But I think the fact that the helmet was stolen is very important for this case."

"Do you know anything about George Smith?"

"No, I don't, but I'll do some research."

"Sherlock, I know you'll solve this case. But you're not authorized for this, and you have no support from the police. This is a German case."

"No, you're wrong, John. It *was* a German case, but now after the death of an Englishman…It is an English case, too."

"Yes… that's right… maybe… but you need legal authorization to be allowed to see the corpse. And we need to see those injuries in order to learn what happened to him."

"Yes, I'll have to ask someone for help."

"Someone who obviously isn't me", I said, hoping he would tell me more.

"Yes, John. As much as I always appreciate your help. Formalities are a thing you can't help me with."

"So then, who can?" I had to ask bluntly.

"You'll see." That was the last answer I got.

"So", I said, changing the subject, "what were you doing back there at the hospital? Apart from leaving me alone to deal with a crying woman?"

"I tried to sneak into one of the offices to get a look at George Smith's file. I was able to find out the exact hour of his death before being detected. He survived for about 35 minutes after the accident. His injures must have been pretty extensive for him to have died within such a short time. I wonder why that is. The other victims haven't died yet. I checked that out, too."

When we arrived at the hotel, Sherlock went straight to his room and I went looking for Lisa, but she wasn't in the hotel at all. I grabbed myself a book and started to read.

Lisa returned an hour later with loads of shopping bags.

"John, I don't want to hear ANYTHING about Sherlock OR the case today. Can you promise me this?" she said before I could get a single word out.

"Oh, please, darling, I promise I won't say anything. And as Sherlock is in his room, we can go out for dinner. What do you think?"

"That's the best idea you've had all day. Let's go. I'm starving."

We went to a authentic Bavarian restaurant again and the meal was very delicious. Lisa and I were happy. The two of us were finally alone. We sat in the restaurant for ages because it was so nice and comfortable. Lisa told me what she had done all day, describing the town's shops and beautiful little cafés. She talked and talked and I listened, eager to absorb everything. I told her how much I liked skiing. She did like it, too, but it was a bit too fast for her taste. This made me laugh because it reminded me how fast my life always seemed to be with Sherlock around. Lisa asked me why I had laughed, but I couldn't tell her. It would have upset her. Instead I told her some joke and we laughed together.

We never mentioned Sherlock or the case throughout the entire evening, but when we arrived back at the hotel, Sherlock was waiting for us in the lobby and Lisa made an unhappy face. I gestured to Sherlock that he shouldn't speak.

But he just grinned and said: "I have done the research regarding George Smith. Want to hear it? It's very interesting."

I immediately knew that this next sentence would be deadly, but I said it anyway, "Yes, tell me everything."

Just as I had guessed, Lisa turned around disappointed and walked away.

"What's wrong with her?" Sherlock asked, but I didn't think he really cared.

"Oh, Sherlock. My relationship with Lisa is going to end soon if I stay near you any longer."

"Poor boy, John. But I have important news for you."

At this very moment Sherlock's phone began to ring and he left to answer it. Apparently this was a call from either his elder brother Mycroft, or Inspector Lestrade from Scotland Yard. So now I had been left on my own.

I sat down, put my head in my hands, and thought about Lisa and our relationship. How had I messed it up so quickly? Would I ever be able to have a good relationship with both Lisa and Sherlock? There were many questions and I had no answers for them.

Sherlock returned from the phone call after about five minutes. I asked him who had called, but he kept it a secret, so I assumed it was related to the "helper" he had mentioned earlier. Well, if he didn't want to tell me, I couldn't change that. So I reminded him why we were both here, "Sherlock, you wanted to tell me what you found out about George Smith."

"Yes, John. Smith was one of the richest men in England. He was the owner of a steel mill that produces guns, tanks, bombs - everything you need to make a fine war. He was born in 1956, studied in Oxford, was a member of Parliament, he worked for the Ministry of Defence, sold lots of his products to the army, married Juliet Howard. They only have this one daughter. Her name is Claire and she was born in 1986. She dislikes her father's business and rumour has it that they haven't talked with each other for years. George Smith made himself many enemies such as environmentalists, members of the peace movement and owners of other weapons industries. "

What a nice man! I was almost a bit glad that he had died.

"So it won't be easy to find his murderer?" I sighed. It seemed as though no one apart from his wife had liked Smith. Many potential murderers.

"Perhaps, but I like difficult cases! Oh, no! I love them!" Sherlock was in his finest mood. So I thought it was best for me to go to bed because the next day would be tiring. I said good night to Sherlock and went to my room.

Chapter Seven: I Am Clever

Sherlock and I were the first to wake the following morning, and I told him that I would only spend half the day with him, because I didn't want to lose Lisa completely. As I informed Lisa of this arrangement, she just nodded and said that it was okay, but of course she would have liked it more if Sherlock had simply disappeared. I could understand that a bit, but this new case had caught my interest so much that I couldn't ignore it any more. In reality I was worried that maybe I would grow addicted to solving crimes, like Sherlock was. Hopefully not, I had to maintain some other priorities, too.

After breakfast, Sherlock and I were on our way to the hospital for the inspection of Smith's body. Sherlock still hadn't told me how we were going to get into the morgue. Lisa had gone skiing without us, but I didn't need to worry, because Mr Gerg, who was still booked, was with her. I hoped the two of them were having a more pleasant time than Sherlock and myself studying a dead man. The way to the hospital seemed shorter than it had the day before.

We soon arrived there and to my surprise, Inspector Lestrade was standing in front of the glass door. Lestrade was a big man, with short grey hair and a grey moustache. He wore a long, furry winter coat, thick clothes, and a woollen scarf; and yet he still seemed to shiver with the cold. When he saw us pull up, he smiled, relieved. "Hello, Sherlock", he nodded in Sherlock's direction and then said to me "John". It bothered me sometimes how people always seemed to see Sherlock before me. We were always "Sherlock and John". They would never say "John and Sherlock", and I guess Sherlock liked this.

"You really can't stay away from a crime scene, can you?" Lestrade said. Apart from his funny comments, Lestrade was a man who took everything very seriously and was also a man of action with whom you were better off not fooling around. He thought very highly of Sherlock and his work, and so it made sense that Sherlock had called him, and not any of the other inspectors of the Yard. They weren't as tolerant and respectful as Lestrade.

„Yeah, you really would think the crimes chase after Sherlock, and not that he chases after them." I replied. "So obviously you are the help Sherlock mentioned."

"Yes, I am. I'm here to set my gorgeous charm loose on the Germans to get you into the morgue to see George Smith's body."

"That is very kind of you," said Sherlock sarcastically.

"But, well, I don't know a single German word apart from "Danke"," admitted Lestrade.

"I will do the talking; you just need to show the papers", Sherlock reassured him.

We then walked to the reception desk and Sherlock spoke to the receptionist, explaining to her that we were from England regarding the autopsy of Mr. George Smith. Looking down at her computer screen, she asked: "Können Sie sich ausweisen?"

"She needs to check our IDs." Sherlock explained. Lestrade pulled some papers which looked very official out of his case and then we all showed our IDs. The secretary scrutinized our papers with utmost precision before telling us to take a seat while she made a phone call.

Soon thereafter, a young female doctor approached us. Or at least I assumed she was a doctor, judging by her white coat. I was curious to see what Sherlock would deduce from her. I guessed her to be about 30 and she was very good looking. Not exactly beautiful like Lisa was, but she was that kind of woman one might like to have a date with. She had curly blond hair falling down to her shoulders and shining brown eyes. Underneath her doctor's coat, I could see a nice purple dress covered in little yellow flowers. She stood very gracefully on her high-heels, making her appear very competent. The doctor introduced herself as "Miss Herrmann". She put an emphasis on the word "miss" and smiled widely at Sherlock. I knew what sort of impression Sherlock's looks made amongst women who didn't know him. The problem was that he knew exactly how to react. He returned her smile and said, "It's absolutely charming to meet you."

He was somehow flirting with her, but this was far better than him attempting to deduce her.

Miss Herrmann brought us into a cellar room which appeared to be a laboratory. The bright light down there was blinding to the eyes and was reflected by white and silver tables. Miss Herrmann opened a sort of cupboard and rolled the dead body lying on a sterile metal bed out under one of the lamps.

This wasn't a pleasant sight. Mr Smith's skull was terribly smashed and it appeared as though every single bone was broken. I heard Lestrade inhale sharply, and he was even more accustomed to this than I was. Miss Herrmann was the pathologist on duty and she pulled her courage together and began to inspect the body in a very professional fashion. She did little talking while she worked, but she kept searching for Sherlock's eyes. When she caught them, she smiled at him and then turned her focus back towards her work. Sherlock and I watched her as she cleaned and examined the body, occasionally handing her some tools. I couldn't handle looking at the corpse constantly, and so I looked around instead. The entire lab seemed to be extremely clean and had been kept in light colours. Staying here all day had to be depressing, and I mentioned that fact to Miss Herrmann.

"Well, at first it scared me, but then I got used to it. Now I welcome the silence down here. And I like the secrets these dead people tell me" She laughed.

"I'm really impressed with how well you do your work", said Sherlock and she blushed.

Then Miss Herrmann said:

"Okay, this is what I can tell you right now. Broken legs, broken skull, and lots of other wounds. The injuries to the legs are very strange. Maybe this happened because of a mistake in the way the skis were bound, or some such. I don't know for sure yet."

"What do you think caused his death?" asked Sherlock.

"The breaking of the skull and the blood loss."

"Do you think he would have survived if he had worn a helmet?"

"Yes, I believe so," answered Miss Herrmann and she inspected Mr Smith's head a bit more. Suddenly she stopped and said "That's odd! Look at those eyes!"

Sherlock, Lestrade, and I leaned in to have a look. The irises had taken on a very strange colour. I couldn't describe it correctly. I couldn't even make out which colour they had been before the accident.

"How has this happened?" asked Sherlock, feigning amazement.

Good question, I thought at first, but then I remembered. Back in the army the pilots had been told a thousand times to be careful with laser pointers. Laser pointers could ruin a person's eyes in an instant and most of the time the people who were using them couldn't be identified because they can be pointed at a victim from a long distance.

"Laser pointer", I said, blurting my thoughts out, and then looked up at Sherlock.

Sherlock made a very strange face. It was a mixture of amazement and shock and I think he was a bit angry, too.

"How do you know this?" he asked sceptically. I told him about the army pilots.

Sherlock still seemed a little off. What was wrong with him? And then I got it.

I had been right! I had known the answer before Sherlock did. I laughed out loud.

"I am right, Sherlock! Oh, I'm so clever! I got it faster than you, right?" Sherlock didn't answer, but his silence was answer enough. Of course this was childish, but I was really very happy to have beaten Sherlock. Even if it was only this one time. Sherlock Holmes, who always spoke with the confidence of being more clever than anyone else, had found himself at a loss and I had been the one to enlighten him. My joy wasn't reasonable, but for that one moment, I couldn't control it.

"I'll allow you to jump up and down if you'd like."

"Sherlock, you know I have beaten you? I am clever, too! You were still thinking about what caused the discolouration of the irises when I had already got it! You have to admit it. I HAVE BEATEN YOU!"

"No, you haven't. Keep dreaming!"

"Oh, no. Admit it now."

"No."

"I'm waiting."

I waited for a while quietly until Sherlock Holmes finally said the words he had never said to anyone in his whole life before: "Alright. I admit it. You have beaten me. But only this once!"

"Fine, Sherlock. I'll take that as the best compliment you've ever given me."

"Hey, boys," interrupted Lestrade, "you may have forgotten, but there's a dead person lying in front of us and you two are fighting over your egos." I immediately shut up and put on a guilty face. This whole show hadn't been particularly respectful towards Mr Smith.

Chapter Eight: The Connection Between The Victims

After our visit to the hospital, my time with Sherlock was over, so I left him and Lestrade and went to the hotel to have a romantic meal with Lisa. We had a fantastic lunch at the hotel restaurant with everything that was needed; several courses of meat, fish, salads and dessert. I knew that this would be quite expensive, but I was feeling guilty for having left Lisa alone, and so I needed to cheer her up, and it worked. Lisa was in the best mood she had been in since our arrival in Bavaria. We laughed and kissed a lot. Sherlock was far from my mind when my mobile suddenly vibrated in my pocket. Luckily, Lisa hadn't noticed it. I excused myself and went to the bathroom, where I read the following message:

I have important news.

Come to the skiing school immediately.

SH

I immediately answered:

No way, Sherlock!

I'm having a good time with Lisa.

Leave us alone and tell me the news later.

JW

I returned to Lisa and showed no sign of my annoyance with Sherlock.

When the lunch was over, I suggested we drink some chilled champagne.

"Well, John," said Lisa, "Why don't we have the champagne delivered straight to our room?"

"Sure," I agreed, as I smiled and raised my arm for the waiter.

A short while later Lisa and I were happily settled in our room. Now we were truly on our own...

Suddenly we heard a knock at the door and someone called out "Room service." Lisa was already standing near the door and opened it, but of course I had recognised the voice at once. It wasn't room service, even though he had made a good show of changing his voice.

"SHERLOCK!" shouted Lisa. She was standing in the doorway, staring at him with wide, angry eyes.

"I want to talk to John, please," said Sherlock.

"Sherlock, I told you to leave us alone!" I screamed into his face. Sherlock showed no reaction and stepped into our room without being invited to do so.

"I have some really important news to tell you." He went on, as if nothing has been said.

"Whatever it is, it can wait until tomorrow."

"Tomorrow will be too late."

"Why?"

"The next victim is due tomorrow."

I was fighting an inner war between listening to Sherlock and punching him in the face, because it was possible that this was all just a trick of his. In the end, my curiosity won. "Okay, give me the information." I said.

"That's it, then" said Lisa in a dangerous tone.

"What is it, Lisa?" I replied.

"You are choosing HIM over me! Again!"

"No, it's not like that. But people are dying...," I tried to defend myself.

"This isn't for the people. This is for him!" She pointed angrily at Sherlock.

"I thought I was your girlfriend, but now I see Sherlock is your everything! When he calls for you, you jump at once! You won't do the same for me! You..." And then, Lisa seemed to have said enough, she couldn't express her anger with words alone any more. Instead she punched me in the face. It hurt more than I would have ever expected. I couldn't move for a moment because I was so astonished. I turned around to Lisa, who had ran past me and was already busy throwing her stuff into a suitcase at high speed, and wanted to say something to her. Before I could get the words out, she had stormed past me again and was gone though the door just seconds later.

Lisa had really left me alone, and I had no chance of bringing her back. Sherlock had destroyed our relationship completely. But had it really been him? Maybe this had all been my fault, because I always do what Sherlock wants me to do, even if it is useless stuff. And I was certainly thrilled about solving crimes with Sherlock. I knew that I needed action in my life, but still...I thought I needed love in my life, too.

I was about to cry out of desperation when I realized that Sherlock was still standing in the doorway. He smiled as if nothing had happened.

"Need a drink?" he asked, holding out a bottle of chilled champagne.

"Yes, please." I sighed. Alcohol was surely not the solution to my problems, but the champagne had already been paid for, so why should I not allow myself one glass to relax?

Sherlock gave me a glass and helped himself to one and then he pointed towards the armchairs. We sat down and I prepared myself for Sherlock's monologue.

"I did some research about all the accidents that occurred last week. As you already know, there have been six accidents within the last six days. This means that each day has one. One victim has died, that was George Smith. We already know about his life. Five are still alive, but two of them are comatose and it's not certain that they will survive their injuries. The other three are still in the hospital. I was able to speak to them and I've gotten all of their names. Getting information about the two people in coma wasn't easy, but I could interview a very talkative nurse.

So let's start with Franz Kramer, 40 years old, born in Munich, has been married four times, no children. His fortune is believed to be about 10 million Euros. He produces a line of luxurious clothing under very bad conditions in Asia. His workers get less then one dollar a day. He now lives an opulent life in his villa near Lenggries and has been skiing since he was four years old. He is currently lying in the hospital with two broken legs, but he should be able to leave without complications. Next- Ludwig Gruber, 67 years old, born in Regensburg, unmarried, no known living relatives and a fortune of about 23 million Euros. He speculates in the stock market for grain and other important foodstuffs. He has made a great deal of money with his trades, but people like him cause the poor people of our world to suffer from starvation because they can't afford the food they need to survive. He is still in a coma. Then we have Maria Ernst. She is 35 years old, born in Berlin, still lives there, married, and has a six year old son, fortune unknown. She came here on holiday. She works for the Ministry of Ecology. She has a concussion and doesn't remember anything that happened within the last week, so it's not certain whether or not her helmet has been stolen, too. But the others have confirmed that they had no helmet at the time the accidents occurred, because it had either been stolen, or had disappeared. Next up -Hugo Lenz, 46 years old, born in Vienna, lives in Munich, married, two daughters, and his fortune is set at about 26 million. He's a shareholder in the development of nuclear energy. He's the other victim who's in a coma. Next in line- Stefan Freiherr von Hohenfelsen, a nobleman, 31 years, was born and still lives in Starnberg. He is married, but has no children. His fortune is great, but unknown, his only job is being a lord and caring for his castles. He has three of them. Von Hohenfelsen is now paraplegic and will be restricted to a wheelchair from now on.

Can you see some connection between all these people?"

I had taken some notes, read through them again, though of course I had noticed something at once: "They are all very rich, or famous, or both."

"Good deduction, John," said Sherlock drily, but I didn't mind. I was used to hearing such comments from him.

"But it's not the only connection. They all live in Germany. Smith does live in England and he's the only victim who has died. They all have common enemies amongst environmentalists or peace movements."

"Do you think the murderer is an *environmentalist?*"

"I suppose so."

"And why do you think the next murder will take place tomorrow?"

"Listen John- Monday, Tuesday, Wednesday, Thursday and Friday all saw accidents without lethal ends, but someone died on Saturday and nothing has happened at all today. So there is a clear scheme. No one dies on working days, because those accidents won't get as much attention. But come Saturday, everyone is on the slope and people will take this death as a warning. Perhaps the police here don't know that these accidents are murders, but we do, and maybe people will believe that skiing has really become more dangerous and they won't do it anymore. But Sunday is the day when God rested and so no work is allowed to be done. Not even the preparation of a murder."

"So our murderer is very religious and doesn't work on Saturdays," I said, summing it all up.

"Yes, you got it."

"And the murderer can't have any regular work, because he needs the time to prepare his murders. How does he do it?"

"I can only guess here. We don't know for sure. First of all, he needs to know his victims very well. He has to know when they come skiing, where they will stay, and where they take their breaks. I think he has made himself some sort of death-list. Next, he follows his victim everywhere and as soon as the helmet is left unattended he grabs it and stashes it. Then he hides just inside the forest and blinds his chosen victim with a laser pointer. It's really quite the miracle that he's always managed to strike the people he intended to harm, and not someone else. Once blinded, the victim crashes into the nearest tree and is brought to the hospital. In Smith's case, the killer even took the time to alter the bindings on his skis in order to keep them from releasing his feet. Because of this, his legs were broken, and he was unable to protect himself from further injury the way the others did. This murderer is really very clever."

"This murderer really scares the hell out of me. How can someone be so cruel?" Just the thought of such a person made me shiver with fear. Where I had initially doubted our actions, now I was one hundred per-cent sure that Sherlock and I were doing the right thing by trying our best to stop this serial killer.

"Only someone who is full of hate. Hate and no other emotion," Sherlock said.

"What's our next job?" I said. I felt the need to do something.

"Lisa is really gone now, isn't she?"

"Yes, she is. Thanks to you." I replied angrily.

"Well, John, it might be my fault, but I know you. You can't pass up a good case, just like me." I kept my mouth shut just then. I thought again about how this murderer was still walking free and adrenaline rushed through my veins.

"So, now that we are on our own, we are free to go to this evening's event in Lenggries."

"Okay, and what is it?"

"It's a skiing equipment fair at the sports centre."

"Why should we go there?"

"Because I'm interested in skiing helmets."

"Really?! You finally want to buy a helmet?"

"Perhaps, but I need to be well informed before I make my choice."

Chapter Nine: At The Ski Equipment Fair

We easily found our way to the fair. It was located about halfway between the hotel and the skiing area. It took place at a great area, at the edge of Lenggries. To my surprise, the fair was in the open air. It appeared to be the parking lot of a supermarket on work-days. The place was crowded, but not as much as one might expect. I once had to remind myself that I was in a small Bavarian town, and not in the city of London. There were lots of advertising posters and a few information booths. Each booth was there to inform visitors about a particular item of skiing gear, but most of the booths were occupied by ski gear-producing companies. I wasn't familiar with very many brands of gear, but the most famous were common to me. Companies like Atomic, Fischer, Elan, Völkel, Head, Rossignol …

I would have loved to stop by each desk and examine the skis, but Sherlock had gone directly to the corner with all the helmets. There were four information desks for each of the skiing helmet companies: Uvex, Giro, Alpina, and Xewow. Sherlock reached the Xewow counter and I followed him. The man behind the counter looked very Bavarian. He wore one of those jackets I had seen many Bavarian men wear - I couldn't recall the proper name, but it seemed to be made of a thick woollen material - a typical Bavarian hat, Lederhosen and a fat stomach, probably full of beer. "Grüß Gott, kann I ihrnan helfan?" Or some such, said he. I understood nothing, but Sherlock answered fluidly in German:

"Hallo, ich möchte mir einen Helm kaufen, aber kenne mich damit überhaupt nicht aus."

„Kein Problem. Ich kenn mich mit Helmen bestens aus! Ich bin der Chef von Xewow, Josef Maier. Hab ich richtig verstanden, der Helm ist für Sie persönlich?"

The man looked from Sherlock, to me, and then inspected Sherlock's head critically.

"Ja, er ist für mich. Allerdings überlegt sich auch mein Freund John hier," Sherlock suddenly pointed at me, „einen Helm zu kaufen. John kommt wie ich aus England, aber er kann kein Deutsch. Wäre es möglich, das Gespräch in Englisch fortzusetzen?"[5]

„Klar, I learned English in school, but I don't have much practice."

The man suddenly switched to English, which was very good for me.

"No problem." Sherlock said, "John, this is Mr Maier. He is the head of Xewow and will inform us about skiing helmets."

Sherlock was actually explaining what was going on. This was very surprising, he usually just did things without talking to me and without thinking of the consequences. I nodded warmly in Mr Maier's direction as he continued "Ehm...there are two different types of helmets, the - let me say - normal style, and the racing helmets. I think you need a normal helmet. I have five different helmets here which you could try on. Look here..."

He showed us all of the helmets lying on his table.

"Mr...ehm," he pointed at Sherlock, "you can try this one"

Mr Maier gave Sherlock a very stylish black helmet that was large in size. Then he handed me a silver helmet in a medium size. I tried it on, even though I already owned a helmet. It fit very well, but I felt my own helmet was more comfortable. Sherlock examined the helmet which had been handed to him very closely, but he didn't put it on. Instead he continued to talk: "Is it true that wearing a helmet can save your life in an accident?"

"Yes, certainly," explained Mr Maier, "you may have heard about all the accidents this week?"

Sherlock nodded.

"None of the victims were wearing a helmet, but if they had been, they would still be alive."

"You seem very sure of this. Do you have any proof?"

"We've informed ourselves very thoroughly about all of these accidents and have run some theoretical tests in order to check how a helmet would have changed the results."

"Has it helped you gain more publicity, and have you been selling more since these accidents occurred?"

"Yes, we've sold about twice the number of helmets within the Lenggries skiing area, but almost nobody cares about the accidents in the other skiing areas."

"But this area is your highest market. You are heavily in debt and made a huge profit in the last week in comparison to all the other weeks. It is a macabre PR gag, but quite effective…"

"What!? Do you mean to say that I have had something to do with the accidents?!"

"No, I don't think so. Still, I had to be sure. My investigation here is finished. Thank you very much, but I won't be buying any of your helmets. Good bye."

Sherlock turned around briskly, leaving Mr Maier standing behind in shock, but then he suddenly screamed "Who are you?"

Sherlock turned around again and quietly said: "I'm Sherlock Holmes, consulting detective."

"Why are you investigating the accidents?"

"Just routine." I couldn't find the sense in his having accused Mr Maier, because I was pretty sure Sherlock had already known that he was innocent before we had even arrived. But how am I to understand Sherlock's methods?

Sherlock and I walked around the fair for a while and pretended to examine the products like normal people. I was fascinated by the number of different styles of skis; from racing skis, to skis that looked a century old. Everything was in that fair.

Suddenly there came a terrible noise.

A group of about twenty people was loudly blowing into whistles and shouting something unintelligible. It was all in German, of course. They were also holding up posters bearing pictures of a pair of skis with a red cross over them along with images of the destroyed landscape. It was immediately obvious that these people were environmentalists.

I asked Sherlock what they were shouting, but when I got no answer, I turned towards him, only to find that he wasn't where I had expected him to be. I searched for him, but suddenly the place had grown very crowded. Chaos was everywhere. It seemed as though the environmentalists had grown aggressive, and more people had begun to shout. The business people standing behind their tables tried to stop the environmentalists, but the environmentalists fought back. Booths were broken, skiing gear was thrown on the ground, and some people screamed. Others were calling for order, but nothing happened.

Worst of all, I had no clue were Sherlock was.

Chapter Ten: Just A Break-In

I tried to calm myself down. *Sherlock is alright, he's okay.* Then I took out my mobile and called him. He wasn't answering his phone. It just kept ringing and ringing, until suddenly the line went dead. I was very frightened because I was alone in a foreign country and there was a street battle taking place in front of my eyes. I kept telling myself that Sherlock was okay. Certainly he was just inspecting everything or following evidence. But still, I didn't feel sure about this. What could I do? Should I go to the police? No, because I wouldn't be able to tell them about Sherlock's investigations. Should I search for him on my own? Too dangerous.

Just as I had decided to go back to the hotel and wait for him there, someone grabbed my arm and pulled me into an alley. I looked up and saw that it was Sherlock.

"Sherlock, you scared the hell out of me!" I shouted.

"Quiet, John," he whispered and pulled me forward to the end of the alley.

"Where are we going?" I asked, trying to keep my voice calm and quiet.

"I'll tell you later. We have to hurry."

He let go of my arm and started to run. I followed, just as I always did. But then I thought about it. Why was I running? I had no idea.

I caught up with Sherlock and this time I grabbed his arm and brought him to a stop.

"What, John?" he snapped.

"I need to know what's going on! First you accuse some German helmet salesman of instigating those accidents, then you simply disappear, and now we are running into something I know nothing about!" I whispered furiously.

"Fine! I think those environmentalists who crashed the fair have something to do with the accidents. So I've decided we're going to their office. But we can only do so as long as they are outside."

"Why? Why do they have to be outside?" I asked.

Sherlock smiled and I knew that what I was thinking was true.

"You know why, John. Will you come and help me?"

I genuinely didn't know what to say. Eventually, I said "You know this is against the law."

"Since when does that bother us?" he asked and kept smiling.

"But Sherlock, seriously? A break-in?"

"Come on, John!"

All I could reply with was "Alright then, we'd better hurry up."

And so we continued running. We ran through slippery and narrow streets. People starred at us. My legs hurt. We had been running an awful lot in those last few days and there was the skiing, too. I yearned for London and the comfort of 221b Baker Street.

After about five more minutes of running, Sherlock came to a halt in front of a huge, typical Bavarian farm. The smell of pigs and cows was heavy in the air and the noises of those animals were clearly coming out of some sort of stall. The stall was old, had dirty glass-windows, and the door was just a few pieces of rotting wood. The farmhouse itself looked very nice, with two huge balconies and traditional paintings of angels and animals. Fortunately we couldn't see anyone around the property, there was a sign on the door which displayed the same heading as the environmentalists' posters.

"How did you know it was here?" I asked.

"On our first evening I took a walk around town and eventually came to this door. I memorized the sign and recognized it as the one from the local environmentalist group. It says: "Our nature is precious, our nature is ours and we fight for it!" Not very creative, I have to admit. Let's see if anyone is at home."

At first I thought Sherlock would simply knock at the door, but then he went to peer into all of the windows of the ground floor. I followed him as quietly as possible. Then we peeked into the stall, but there were no human beings to be found, just about ten cows and a few pigs. They had lots of space, and for animals, this was surely a nice home. For them, the odour wasn't bad. Maybe they even liked the smell.

"That's what they want to see everywhere", Sherlock explained as he closed the door, "They want all the animals in the world to live happily, and all of the mountains kept natural for the cows to graze on the slopes, but the skiing destroys all of this. Skiing is the most environmentally damaging sport. Even worse than motorsports."

"I didn't know that" I admitted, startled.

"That's not surprising. Nearly no one does. That is why this group has tried to raise awareness. It hasn't worked. Skiing tourism is important for many regions along the Alps. As a result, the group became violent and radical. Sending out blackmail letters and stuff like that. I've researched them with my phone. Come on then." Sherlock crept closer to a window that seemed to be slightly ajar. Within seconds he had cracked it open widely and was inside the house. I hesitated for a moment, making sure no one was there to watch me. Then I went after him.

The house was huge. It was two stories tall and was made up of about ten big rooms. Sherlock needed my help to find what we were looking for. The window turned out to be the window of a bathroom. Luckily, the toilet seat had been closed; otherwise we would have been soaked with water. I struggled to my feet and looked back through the window once more, but all was quiet.

Sherlock was already in the hall. I followed him. We went up the stairs and were soon in an office. In the middle of the room was an old desk with a mess of papers on top. The walls were covered with bookshelves full of binders. It was the perfect place to hide a single piece of paper. A particular piece of paper with information - that was what we were looking for, I guessed.

"Sherlock", I whispered, cautiously trying not to touch anything, "What do you expect to find here? They won't plan everything out and just keep the notes here, will they?"

"No, of course not. I don't even think they all know what the plan is. The group consists primarily of thirty stable members. This is the house of the founder, Konrad Bäcker. Maybe we can get a list of all the primary members or something like that." Sherlock put on a pair of latex gloves and searched through the papers on the desk.

"And what if the murderer isn't a member of this group at all?"

"Well, then we will go on searching for someone who has the same motives, but is maybe in another organisation...I think we need to check the computer."

I let out a sigh of relief. Thanks to modern technology, we didn't have to search every single folder.

"Sherlock, are you sure they won't come back soon?" I grew more nervous, as more time trickled by.

"Relax, John." He had already turned the computer on and was searching through the desktop. His fingers were moving very quickly over the keyboard for a while, but then he stopped before continuing to type. It probably only took about a minute, but it seemed like hours.

"I got it!" He exclaimed, delighted, and quickly took a photo with his Smartphone. He turned the computer off and put everything in order. Well, at least he was putting things back the way they had been, which was in a state of complete disorder.

"Okay, out we go!" he said and we ran back to the bathroom. Again, we had to stand on the toilet seat as we climbed out of the window. I landed ungracefully on my arse. Sherlock gave me his hand and pulled me up just in time. Seconds later, a voice shouted: "Grüß Gott, was suchans hier?"

All the blood drained from my face and I was unable to move out of shock. Damn it, we'd been caught. But Sherlock just turned around, smiled, and calmly said in German: "Entschuldigen Sie, wir sind Engländer und haben uns nur ein bisschen umgesehen. Wir gehen gleich wieder."[6]

The voice laughed, and I realised, it was a female. Then she said something again, this time in English: "Oh, it's alright. May I give you a tour around? This isn't my property, but it's the farm of a friend of mine."

"No, thank you. We've got to go now. Good bye." Sherlock said, also switching to English. Then he took my arm, guiding me away, and I was luckily able to move again. Curious, I looked back at the woman; she appeared to be in her late twenties and smiled as we walked away.

We stopped as soon as we were out of sight.

"That was close!" I said, laughing, because I was so glad that I wouldn't need to go to a German prison.

"Indeed it was!" Sherlock agreed and joined in the laughter. "But we have what we needed."

"Show me," I urged. Sherlock handed me his phone and I looked at the list. There were 34 names, most of them sounded German, and some seemed to be Eastern-European.

"Well, now we have all these names. What are we going to do with them? Interrogate each of these people? They could be spread all over the world."

"No. We will find another way to catch the murderer. But once we have him, we'll already know his name."

"So, we have just broken into a house for nothing?"

"Maybe, maybe not. We'll see."

Chapter Eleven: The Kitten Helmet

The next morning Sherlock and I had breakfast in the hotel restaurant. To my enormous surprise, Miss Herrmann showed up in our hotel and joined us. She gave me the final report of her inspection of Mr Smith's body, but there wasn't much new information. The next surprise was that Sherlock had invited her the day before to stay with us the rest of the week. Of course Veronica, that was her first name, had agreed. I welcomed her company because she was very nice and funny, but it would have been much better with Lisa. Veronica hadn't brought any skiing gear. It turned out she was from Berlin. We decided to go to a shop to rent the needed equipment. She already knew how to ski, so we had no need for Mr Gerg's lessons any more. I called him and cancelled all of the remaining lessons without giving him a reason, but I promised him that he would get his money anyway and he was fine with it. Sherlock had been right that first day. He wasn't particularly eager to be a skiing instructor; he cared more for money.

After breakfast we entered the shop where we could rent Veronica's skiing gear. As we walked around the shop, looking for stuff in her size, I gestured to Sherlock that I needed to talk to him. We went into a quiet corner where we thought Veronica couldn't see or hear us.

"Why is she with us?" I whispered and looked around cautiously, "you are not seriously interested in her, are you?" My tone implied that I would be very, *very* surprised if Sherlock had any feelings for the poor girl. Sherlock had never shown any interest in women.

"Of course not!" he replied and smiled "but I need her for the case."

"What?" I was nearly shouting now. "You can't get her involved in your business. Lisa was nearly killed once because of you. I won't let you put Veronica in danger like that."

"It's not dangerous at all. I just need her to wear a special helmet so we can watch the murderer steal it. But I'll take care of her. Nothing will happen to her. I might not be interested in her, but I'm not so cold hearted as to let her die for me."

With that said, our conversation ended. Veronica had found us in the corner and came to show us a pair of skis she had chosen. They were in very good condition and seemed to be the right size. A clerk made the appropriate adjustments and we tried to find the other gear she would need.

Sherlock pulled a helmet from a shelf and showed it to Veronica. It was bright pink with pictures of lovely little kittens. Why would Sherlock need her to wear such a ridiculous helmet? A kitten helmet?

"What do you think, Veronica? Isn't it cute?" Sherlock asked.

His voice was gentle. She seemed uncertain what to do. I thought she wouldn't want to appear too girlish, but she certainly loved kittens, just like any woman I had known. In the end, she took the helmet in her hands and examined it closely.

"Why don't you try it on?" suggested Sherlock.

She did. Not only did the outside match her well, but the size seemed to be right, too.

"Oh, this helmet is perfect for you," said Sherlock charmingly and Veronica blushed.

"What else do you need?" I asked in an attempt to change the topic.

We had soon found everything Veronica needed for skiing and we set off to the slopes.

Veronica and Sherlock chatted the whole morning about her work in the morgue. Most of the time I was too disgusted to listen. Veronica skied very well for not being a local and we were once again on the highest slopes.

At lunchtime Sherlock suggested we eat something in a hut. A hut like this was a typical building in the area along the Alps. It was made mostly of wood and appeared to be glued to the mountainside. In winter, snow was hanging of the inclined roof, making the hut part of the beautiful landscape. The hut we entered was pretty large and looked luxurious. It seemed to be built for the tourists rather than for the locals who used to live on the mountains all summer long taking care of their cows. There were more foreigners than in the other huts in which we had been so far. There was even a brass band. Many people chatted loudly, which made it difficult for us to understand each other.

We sat down and ordered something to drink. Then we took a look at the menu and decided on what we wanted to eat. I was beginning to feel like I really could get used to Bavarian food. Veronica and I chatted while waiting for the waitress. Sherlock periodically joined the conversation by making a comment, but most of the time he just stayed very alert and watched his surroundings. He had departed from his earlier talkative mood and had again become the observing detective. I tried hard not to worry about what he might see here and I made sure Veronica's attention was kept focused on me. I could not let her ask what Sherlock was doing. It might have destroyed his plan. We received our food, and while we ate, Sherlock continued to look around. At the very moment I wanted to tell him that he was behaving impolitely by staring at people and give him a warning about how obvious he was, he rose from his seat and passed to the other side of the restaurant. He paused there for just a few seconds, and then returned to our table.

"What was that about?" I asked curiously.

"I just wanted to be sure of something."

"Could you please explain to me why you stood up without an obvious reason?" I whispered while Veronica was talking to someone else.

"I always have good reasons for doing these things and they are obvious, too. You see, John, but you don't observe." This mysterious answer was all I got. "You have your gun with you, haven't you?" Sherlock added quietly. I nodded and showed him my gun hidden in my jacket pocket. He smiled satisfied. After my very first adventure with Sherlock I had begun to always take a gun with me. I had the feeling we soon would come to a turning point in this case.

Soon afterwards we finished our lunch and put on our skiing gear. I was already ready for the slope when I noticed that Veronica was looking desperate.

"What's the problem?" I asked kindly.

"I can't find the kitten helmet."

"I'll help you," I said, and immediately started to look around, but I could see no sign of the cute pink helmet. "Come on, Sherlock. Help us. It has to be somewhere…" I said absentmindly.

"No, it isn't in the hut anymore, but I think I know where we have to look," replied Sherlock.

"What!?" exclaimed Veronica.

"Come with me outside."

We followed Sherlock, curious. Once outside the hut, he looked around and was able to detect some footprints not far away. He waved us towards him.

"We just need to follow these footprints."

"And they'll lead us to Veronica's helmet", I said sceptically.

"Indeed they will. But, Veronica, this trip may be dangerous; it would be safer for you to return to the hut."

"No way. I want to know what happened to the kitten helmet."

Sherlock considered this for a moment and then said "Fine. Let's go. But be quiet. Very quiet."

Veronica and I nodded in agreement and we all set off together after the footprints. They led us deep into the forest behind the hut. The forest was boreal and snow hung heavily from every tree. This made the light very dim.

We had been walking for more than quarter of an hour when Sherlock suddenly got tense. He gestured to me that I should get my gun ready to fire and I did so. Veronica gasped when she saw the gun. She looked terrified. Sherlock's look seemed to say, "I told you it could be dangerous".

Then we moved on. All of a sudden there weren't any more trees. We found ourselves on the edge of a small meadow. In the middle was a single tree whose branches were hung round with black, white, and silver objects. One was even pink. My immediate thought was that this was some sort of late Christmas tree, but then I realised that those things were indeed… skiing helmets.

There were skiing helmets hanging in a tree. And there were seven of them. "The seven missing helmets," I said, speaking my thoughts out loud.

"Gorgeous, isn't it, John? The murderer stole the helmets to make sure that his victims die."

"Are you saying…?" Veronica looked very confused and anxious, "Do you think I was supposed to be the next victim?"

"No, Veronica. Your helmet wasn't supposed to hang there. The murderer made the mistake I was hoping for. Well, it was the mistake I planned for him to make." Sherlock was finally launching his explanation of all this.

"Don't you remember the rich lady back at the hut? She had exactly the same helmet. I noticed this yesterday and informed myself about her. Susanne Peter, she wanted to expand this skiing area into an even bigger one. Local farmers protested because she wanted to take their land. Environmentalists protested because all of this would have destroyed nature even more. You see, she was similar to the other victims. I immediately knew she would be the next.

"So I took action. I located the same kitten helmet in the rental store and made sure Veronica got it. Back in the hut, I swapped the two helmets and once Veronica's was gone I put the other in its original place. But what's still a mystery to me, is why the murderer has done so many things to avoid any suspicion that these "accidents" might be murders, and yet he displays the helmets very obviously."

"Sherlock, don't you know who the murderer is yet?" I asked, confused because his deduction of the case had dripped off so quickly.

"No, we've come too late. But we'll trap him tomorrow. John, you will surely accompany me, won't you?"

"Of course," I agreed. My adrenaline was running high in the anticipation of our next killer-hunt. Sherlock smiled. He liked the idea of catching the evil, just as I did. He turned to Veronica and his face grew serious "But the trapping is nothing that a lady such as yourself, Veronica, should be involved in. So please stay safe in the hotel."

"Sss...sure", stammered Veronica and blushed, I believed because Sherlock had called her a lady.

Chapter Twelve: Catching The Murderer

The next morning Sherlock and I got up pretty early; we left the hotel soon afterwards and arrived at the meadow with the helmet-tree in silence, without leaving more footprints than the day before. We hid behind some bushes and waited there for a long time without saying a single word. The silence around us was palpable; there was nothing to be heard except for the occasional cry of a bird. When the sun had risen high into the sky, we finally heard heavy footsteps approaching us. Moments later, a figure appeared at the edge of the meadow. The figure looked around, cautiously, but seemed confident that the area was clear of people, not detecting us in our shelter. The man stepped out from the shadow of the trees. He was wearing black winter outdoor clothes, but I couldn't make out what his face looked like because of his hat and scarf. He carried a helmet with him, which he hung up on the tree, just like the other seven. It looked exactly the same as the helmet Veronica had been wearing the day before. Sherlock had been right. Susanne Peter was to be the next victim. But we were here now to prevent any more planned accidents.

I exchanged a look with Sherlock. He nodded and rose from our hideout. I followed his movement. I readied my gun in a flash, aiming for the man under the helmet-tree.

"Stop!" shouted Sherlock. "Keine Bewegung! Wir sind bewaffnet!"[7]

The killer froze. Slowly he began to turn around to face us. We still couldn't make out much of his face. I recognised something funny about his features, as his face twisted into an evil smile, but I couldn't put my finger on it. Then we heard the voice, a female voice: "Nice to finally meet you, Mr Holmes!"

I was shocked. Twice over. The murderer in front us, whom we had always considered to be a man, was actually a woman. Not only that, *she also knew Sherlock.*

I glanced between her and Sherlock, confused. He stared at her; eyes narrowed, as he tried to process what was going on. She, on the other hand, looked quite relaxed and happy.

"I know you don't know me at all. But I have heard a lot about you, Sherlock Holmes." The murderess went on.

"Who are you?" asked Sherlock, still pointing his gun at her.

"Oh, come on! You know who I am. Well, you at least know why I've done all this and you have a list of names to choose from."

She pointed upwards to the helmets in the tree. Sherlock had been right. She was a member of the environmental group whose headquarters we'd broken into. Perhaps she was even the woman who had seen us. But I wasn't sure. That woman hadn't worn a scarf or a hat. But the smile, yes, maybe that was the same.

"You are a fanatic environmentalist," Sherlock said at last.

"Yes, I am. And I think I have achieved my goal now. These five people lying in the hospital will remember my act forever and, well... Smith, he deserved it. He was the most evil of them all. I'm a bit sorry I didn't get to Susanne Peters. But I knew you were here to catch me, Mr Holmes. It was just a question of time until we met. And, oh, I've enjoyed the thrill of working while being chased. But I'm a little bit disappointed that you needed four full days to figure out my plans. I really made it so easy for you. I even purposely ran into you."

She paused for a moment and glanced at Sherlock expectantly.

"I do remember that encounter at the headquaters. And I drew the right conclusions; I just needed to prove them. Now I have you under my control. We'll put you in jail for the rest of your life."

He took a few steps towards her, gun still in hand. She stepped back.

"Oh, really?! You know that's all I ever wanted."

"No, it won't be like anything you expect it to be. I'll make sure of this. I don't like anyone who wanders around and kills people in cold blood. But I *particularly hate* anyone who tries to fool me."

Sherlock moved in closer and closer. They were just a few inches apart now. The murderess had moved backwards as much and far as she could until her back was pressed against the tree. She was trapped. Just as we had planned her to be.

"Do you really think I fear you?" she asked. But the question seemed quite ironic because her voice was shaking hysterically.

I had no clue what was going on, but I felt sure Sherlock had everything under control. He had a gun, while she was without a weapon.

"Well, you should. Come on, John, we know enough to get her put on trial. Let's bring her to the police."

I immediately obeyed and jumped towards her, but her reaction was too fast. She turned around and started to climb the tree. We tried to pull her back to the ground, but she was too skilled at climbing. Within seconds she was out of our reach. So we stood there like hunters waiting for our prey to leave its hideout.

"You won't get me!" she cried from up in the tree.

Sherlock didn't respond.

"What do we do now? Wait until she falls down?" I asked.

"Yes, we wait and chat a little more."

"Why don't we call the police right now?"

"Because I'd like to chat first and she won't escape us here."

"What good will that do?"

I was confused. As far as our history had gone, talking to criminals hadn't always been a good idea. This had always gotten us into trouble. But I was also curious as to how she knew Sherlock and what she had planned. It was as if I had said my thoughts out loud because Sherlock suddenly said: "We are going to figure this out."

He looked up into the tree and shouted "Tell me how you know me!"

"Oh, someone told me about you. Someone even more brilliant than I."

"Who?"

"James. My dear cousin James!"

Chapter Thirteen: James Moriarty's Cousin

My world froze in place. James?! This name had been burned into my brain. James Moriarty! James was the evil criminal mastermind, who had wanted to kill Sherlock and me. Even though James is a very common name, there could be no doubt that the murderess was speaking of Moriarty. I told myself that it shouldn't have been that much of a shock. Every recent criminal adventure had lead to Moriarty in some way or another. Still, I had just never thought of Moriarty having a family. But now her craziness didn't surprise me anymore. I decided that it had to be in the genes, and I understood now why there had been something familiar in her features. There was an awful silence that I had to break so I asked in the faint hope this was just an illusion "You are really James Moriarty's cousin?"

"Sure, Johnny."

There it was, the final proof: "Johnny". The stupid nickname Moriarty had given me.

"I'm pleased to meet some part of James' family," Sherlock said at last.

He seemed calm and indifferent, but I knew what was going on in his brain. Even though the murderess was unaware of it, she was a good source for information about Moriarty. Sherlock just needed to act clever. But then, he always managed that.

"Well, I suppose you're name isn't Moriarty, is it?" asked Sherlock.

"I like the name Moriarty and it's a shame it isn't mine. No, I just have this stupid German name: Johanna Lindlbaur."

"How closely related are you to James?"

"Well, he's the son of my mother's sister. We visited each other nearly every school holiday. I have lots of cousins, but James was the only one I liked. We have the same sense of humour; we have the same hobbies…"

"Hobbies? What, like killing people?" I interrupted.

"Well, no. When we were younger we just created criminal masterplans. We stole and blackmailed to get loads of sweets. And we never got caught. We were a good team. We still sort of are. But he made organised criminality into his profession, and I became an environmentalist. You know, there are many people who think all you have to do is organise demonstrations and shout out for the rights of animals and nature. But that's not enough. So I reached for harsher measures."

"What has Moriarty got to do with all this?"

"I have been planning this for a long time because it's not easy to arrange all of these accidents without raising suspicion. So I asked James for help and he did help me. He gathered all of the information about the rich and influential. In the beginning, I just wanted to kill ordinary people. But James was right. Celebrities raise more attention. So, some days ago everything was arranged and I wanted to start my painful and deadly mission. And then James called me and told me you were coming, Mr Holmes. And... well, this sort of changed things, because at first I had considered telling the police what I had done after the fifth victim. But with you here I just *had* to wait for you to catch me."

"It's honourable to be caught by *the great* Sherlock Holmes, isn't it? But now I ruin your plan. Because no one will know that I was involved."

Sherlock reached into his pocket for his mobile. A triumphant look on his face, he showed me the display. It said "*Saved recording*". I hadn't noticed him recording the murderess' confession. Yet, there it was on his Smartphone, every single word Johanna Lindlbaur had said.

Chapter Fourteen: Surprises

Johanna Lindlbaur was locked up in jail. Sherlock had called the police and they had violently pulled her down from the tree. Thanks to Sherlock recording her confession, there was no way out for her. But then, she was related to Moriarty, which meant anything was possible.

A while later, Lestrade came and checked everything and wrote a few reports for Scotland Yard on behalf of George Smith. His was still sort of an English case, too and so Scotland Yard needed to be involved.

We had booked the hotel for one whole week, so we decided to stay two days longer. When we returned to the hotel after having spoken with the police, we found that Veronica had been worried that we might have been killed. Like me, she was glad it was otherwise. I had to admit, though, that this wasn't the most dangerous case Sherlock and I had ever solved. Veronica had never heard of Sherlock Holmes before, but after this affair she had googled him and found out that he was a famous detective and had begun to like him even more.

I told Sherlock that he needed to end this, and he did. Veronica had come into the hotel for breakfast once more. She had been very cheery when she entered. Then Sherlock told her that the whole reason why he had invited her to come with us skiing had been that he had needed a woman to wear the kitten helmet. He made it clear that every time he had said Veronica was special or made a compliment, he had just wanted her to stay until his plan had worked out. While he told her this, Veronica's smile had dropped from her face. I saw her blink away some tears. "A game? That's what it is for you, isn't it? Catching a murderess is a game and seducing a woman is just another game you play." Even though she hadn't known him that long, she was right about him. And then, Sherlock made it all worse by saying: "Yes, it is fun for me, these games. But you have to admit, you really weren't that hard to get. Someone had just dumped you, when we first met. You were heartbroken, looking for someone, and I just came along dragging you into an adventure. Really you should thank me…"

At that point I had simply pulled Sherlock out of the room. "Just shut up, you are making this worse," I had snapped at him and had returned to a crying Veronica. "I'm sorry," I said, "I'm really sorry, I should have warned you, I guess, but I didn't know…"

"Oh, it's alright, John. I don't blame you. I always fancy the wrong men. Anyway it was nice to have met you, but I want to be alone now. Good bye." Veronica left. I really hoped she would find someone someday who truly loved her. She was such a nice person. She deserved it.

Much to my surprise, Sherlock's elder brother Mycroft visited us the day before our departure. Sherlock looked very puzzled about his arrival. "Mycroft, what are you doing here *in person*? This case isn't a matter of national importance."

Mycroft raised an eyebrow. "This case is not a matter of national importance, but *you* are, brother. I just wanted to make sure you behave yourself with the German police and don't make a show of it," said Mycroft sternly.

"There's nothing to worry about. Lestrade is the genius who will take all the glory, as always."

"Lestrade?" Mycroft was startled.

So was I. Sherlock, didn't want to accept the glory for catching a murderer? He was famous for his great adventures and even though he didn't want to be in newspapers, I still thought he liked the attention he got.

"Well, it was the murderess' plan that I catch her so that *she* could show off and get more publicity. But as I said, I'm disrupting her gorgeous plans because no one except for you knows that I was the one who caught her. To make sure everybody really believes this, Lestrade and the German Police will say *they* found everything out. So, Mycroft, don't worry. It will be as though I were never here."

The pieces fell together in my mind. Now I understood Sherlock's behaviour towards the police. Now I could see that he had done this for a greater reason. He didn't accept the glory, but he did take the victory. That was much better. Johanna Lindlbaur was now just another criminal caught by the police. Not a criminal caught by Sherlock Holmes.

The skiing trip had been completely different from what I had expected it to be. I had still skied a lot, and the days had been very exciting. Perhaps a bit *too* exciting. But I had learned my lesson: Sherlock *didn't* always follow the criminals, but they sort of followed him, too. I regretted what had happened with Lisa, but I still hoped there might be a way to sort things out.

After exactly one week in Germany, Sherlock and I returned to 221B Baker Street. It was a pleasure to be home again. Mrs Hudson was already awaiting us with tea and biscuits.

"Oh, boys!" she greeted us "I missed you! Tell me how it was!"

She hugged us warmly and smiled. It was such a nice way to come home.

"Yes, it was very nice. We took some photos for you and I printed them so you can see them on paper, the old fashioned way."

Sherlock handed her a pile of photos.

"Oh, thank you, dear."

Mrs Hudson put on her glasses and examined the pictures. Suddenly she screamed and the pile of photos fell to the floor. Reflexively, I picked them up again and looked at them. They definitely weren't the photos I would give someone after a skiing trip: A picture of the dead Mr George Smith, the helmet tree, the scene of Mr. Smith's accident...

"Oh, no, Sherlock!" I exclaimed, "I'm so sorry, Mrs Hudson. *These* are the photos I took for you...here look... Sherlock has indeed been skiing..."

Once the shock had faded, Mrs Hudson looked at my photos. She and I laughed a lot over Sherlock skiing in his long, billowing coat.

Meanwhile, Sherlock had sat down in front of the computer, and was checking to see if he had another case yet.

"John," his voice sounded hoarse.

"What?" I asked.

He pointed at the screen of his computer. I leaned over and read the email that was displayed there:

Hey Sherlock,

Nice try, catching my dear little cousin. I hope you never believed she would stay in prison for long. With my connections and cousinly love towards her...she will be a free woman soon...joining me on my mission. She really is great, isn't she? I gave her the opportunity to play with you and she has proven herself to be worthy of my trust. But I have to say, you haven't proven yourself to be as good as everyone says. Five days, Sherlock, five days... we both know you can do better than that.

So let's play again!

Greet Johnny from me, will you?

JM

Also from MX Publishing

MX Publishing is the world's largest specialist Sherlock Holmes publisher, with over a hundred titles and fifty authors creating the latest in Sherlock Holmes fiction and non-fiction.

From traditional short stories and novels to travel guides and quiz books, MX Publishing cater for all Holmes fans.

The collection includes leading titles such as _Benedict Cumberbatch In Transition_ and _The Norwood Author_ which won the 2011 Howlett Award (Sherlock Holmes Book of the Year).

MX Publishing also has one of the largest communities of Holmes fans on Facebook with regular contributions from dozens of authors.

www.mxpublishing.com

Also from MX Publishing

Sherlock Holmes Short Story Collections

Sherlock Holmes and the Murder at the Savoy

Sherlock Holmes and the Skull of Kohada Koheiji

Look out for the new novel from Mike Hogan
– *The Scottish Question.*

www.mxpublishing.com

Also from MX Publishing

Our bestselling books are our short story collections;

'Lost Stories of Sherlock Holmes' , 'The Outstanding
Mysteries of Sherlock Holmes', The Papers of Sherlock
Holmes Volume 1 and 2, 'Untold Adventures of Sherlock
Holmes' (and the sequel 'Studies in Legacy) and 'Sherlock
Holmes in Pursuit', 'The Cotswold Werewolf and Other Stories
of Sherlock Holmes' – and many more......

www.mxpublishing.com

Also from MX Publishing

"Phil Growick's, 'The Secret Journal of Dr Watson', is an adventure which takes place in the latter part of Holmes and Watson's lives. They are entrusted by HM Government (although not officially) and the King no less to undertake a rescue mission to save the Romanovs, Russia's Royal family from a grisly end at the hand of the Bolsheviks. There is a wealth of detail in the story but not so much as would detract us from the enjoyment of the story. Espionage, counter-espionage, the ace of spies himself, double-agents, double-crossers...all these flit across the pages in a realistic and exciting way. All the characters are extremely well-drawn and Mr Growick, most importantly, does not falter with a very good ear for Holmesian dialogue indeed. Highly recommended. A five-star effort."

The Baker Street Society

Endnotes

---

[1]   Good morning, my friend John Watson requested an instructor. His name is Mr Gerg.

[2]   Just a moment, please.

[3]   "Ami" is a very colloquial and a bit derogatory (has a somewhat negative connotation) word for American people

[4]   May I help you?

[5]   My friend, John wants to buy a helmet, too. John can't speak English. Maybe we can continue our conversation in English?

[6]   Please excuse us. We are English and we were just looking around. We'll leave immediately.

[7]   Don't move! We are armed!